To Lulu
—E.S.

In memory of my father, Claus Hilb, who night after night
told my sisters and me the most wonderful stories in the world.
—N.H.

ZONDERKIDZ

Nora's Ark
Copyright © 2012 by Eileen Spinelli
Illustrations © 2012 by Nora Hilb

Requests for information should be addressed to:

Zonderkidz, 5300 Patterson Ave SE, Grand Rapids, Michigan 49530

Library of Congress Cataloging-in-Publication Data
Spinelli, Eileen.
 Nora's ark / written by Eileen Spinelli ; illustrated by Nora Hilb.
   p.   cm.
   Summary: When the weatherman predicts rain, young Nora builds an ark just like
Noah's—almost.
   ISBN 978-0-310-72006-5 (hardcover)
   [1. Noah's ark—Fiction. 2. Play—Fiction. 3. Imagination—Fiction.] I. Hilb, Nora, ill.
II. Title.
PZ7.S7566Nor 2013
[E]—dc23   2011023551

Editor: Barbara Herndon
Art direction & design: Jody Langley

Printed in China

12 13 14 15 16 17 /LPC/ 6 5 4 3 2 1

Nora's Ark

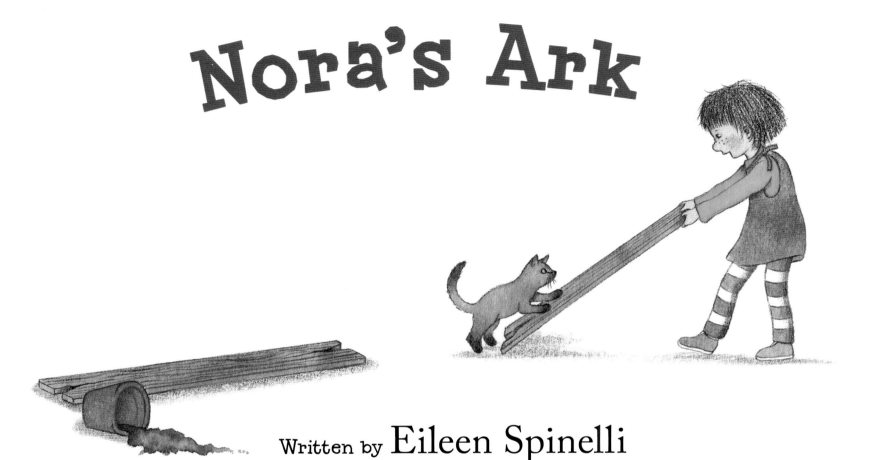

Written by Eileen Spinelli

Illustrated by Nora Hilb

ZONDERkidz

ZONDERVAN.com/
AUTHORTRACKER
follow your favorite authors

The weatherman predicted rain.
So Nora built an ark.
Just like Noah.

Well ...
not *just* like Noah.

Nora's ark was built from
one broken attic chair,
two dusty wooden boxes,
and three old fence slats.
Nora's ark was smaller.

There was room for Nora
and Nora's little brother, Franky,
and Nora's best friend, Lily.
The rest of the space had to be saved for the animals.

Nora welcomed the animals
just like Noah.
Two by two.

Well...

not *just* like Noah.

Noah welcomed elephants, tigers, and giraffes.
There were no elephants, tigers, and giraffes on Elm Street
where Nora lived.

So Nora welcomed
two spiders,
two goldfish,
two cats,
and two toy monkeys.

After a few minutes, the cats left.
They had better things to do than wait for rain.

Next, Franky left to take his afternoon nap.

Then Lily left for her dentist appointment.

But Nora stayed.
She waited for the rain to fall
just like Noah.

Well...
not *just* like Noah.

Nora ate a bag of pretzels while she waited.
(Perhaps Noah ate a fig.)

She painted her toenails.

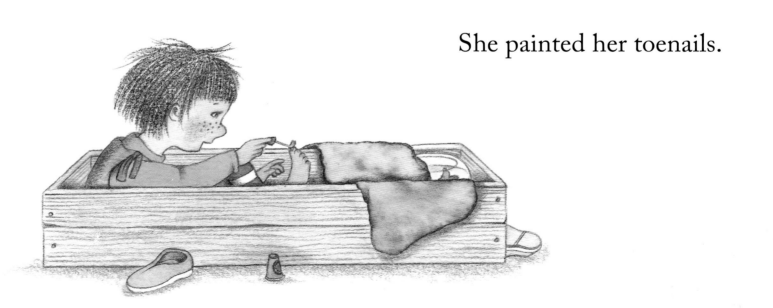

She played with the toy monkeys until
their batteries ran out.

Finally the rain began.
Just like in Noah's time.

Well...
not *just* like in Noah's time.

It didn't rain on Elm Street for
forty days and forty nights.
It only rained for about
forty minutes, maybe thirty-five.

But Nora tended the animals every minute
just like Noah.

Well...
not *just* like Noah.

Nora did leave the ark once,
to get a popsicle for herself from the freezer.

After a while Nora's big sister, Kayla, poked her head into the ark.

"What are you doing?" she asked.

Nora grinned. "I'm being just like Noah. I'm floating on the flood."

Kayla laughed. "There isn't any flood. All I see are a couple of puddles. And anyway, it's dinnertime."

"Okay."

Nora walked down the
box-lid ramp of the ark.

The rain had stopped.
The air smelled fresh.
The clouds were gone.
Nora saw a rainbow.
It reached wonderfully,
from one side of the sky
to the other.

It made her heart sing …
just like Noah's.